THE MAGIC STAIRCASE

by

Marilyn Morrison

RoseDog Books

PITTSBURGH, PENNSYLVANIA 15238

RoseDog Books
585 Alpha Drive, Suite 103
Pittsburgh, PA 15238
Visit our website at www.rosedogbookstore.com

ISBN: 978-1-4809-9659-5
eISBN: 978-1-4809-9636-6

THE MAGIC STAIRCASE

Ella loved playing in the sandbox with her brother.

They sometimes found pennies that were buried there by their mother.

Ella and David searched for buried treasure,

and one day they found it, and it was beyond measure!

On a warm, sunny day they were digging in the sand,

when a cool wind blew and clouds came rolling in.

As they looked up in the sky, they couldn't believe their eyes.

A large winding staircase was spiraling down,

down,

down,

to their surprise!

Shocked and alarmed, they jumped hand in hand

as the staircase unfolded and touched down in their sand!

They turned and looked up at the staircase so high.

It went up, up, up, high up in the sky!

David watched for a while and said with a smile,

"Let's see where this goes!"

And he jumped on the ladder and up he arose.

Ella was cautious and wanted to wait,

but David was already well on his way!

As David climbed higher,

Ella tried to catch up.

"Come down right now," Ella said,

climbing as fast as she could climb up!

Touching the clouds, David was climbing so fast.

Climbing right behind him, Ella was AGHAST!

As they entered the clouds, it was beautiful and bright.

Ella looked down and saw nothing but white.

She didn't know what to do, or how to stop him in time,

so higher Ella went, higher she climbed.

Ella bumped into her brother; suddenly he had stopped.

David had reached a GOLDEN DOOR at the top.

They both were wondering what was inside;

Ella knocked on the door, afraid of what they would find.

David quickly knocked also, but harder this time.

Ella's heart beat faster as the doorbell chimed.

The door began to open and to their surprise,

a beautiful princess led them inside!

As they entered the room,

they couldn't believe their eyes!

They were surrounded by snacks

of every kind and every size!

There were shelves of cookies, bags of popcorn,

candy bars, suckers, bubble gum and sweets;

there were tootsie rolls and gummy bears, pie and cake, too!

There was no end to all of the snacks they could view!

Ella and David turned slowly and saw

candy was everywhere, on every wall.

The princess told them to choose snacks to eat!

Both kids were excited, and both grabbed a treat!

They ate popcorn, peanuts, and a bag of jelly beans;

they ate M&Ms, tootsie rolls, and then candy canes.

They ate cookies, and with it, drank a tall glass of milk.

"I'm so full," David said. "I feel kind of ick…"

Ella rubbed her tummy, "I can't eat anymore!"

She sat down but jumped up when she spotted a GREEN DOOR!

David ran toward the door, the princess opened it wide.

They couldn't wait to see what was inside!

"TOYS!" shouted David. "There are toys everywhere!"

As Ella peeked in, she could see a stuffed bear.

There were toy trains, whistles, and dolls that could talk;

there were airplanes, cars, and big, red dump trucks.

There were cars you could race, and cars you could ride.

David jumped into one and began to drive!

There were games and play-doh; there were marbles and jacks.

There were yoyos, and balls, and bicycles on racks.

Everywhere they looked they saw shelves of toys,

and the princess said, "Feel free to make lots of noise!"

Ella ran to the dolls, grabbed a stroller to walk.

David ran toward the train, then the trucks, then saw chalk!

They played, and they played till they couldn't play anymore,

out of breath, they sat down… then spotted a BLUE DOOR!

They wondered what wonders could be inside.

The princess opened the door really wide.

Both children gasped because they loved to read,

and they saw books everywhere, THEY DANCED WITH GLEE!

Ella eagerly went through the door, followed closely by her brother.

They wanted to see what books they could discover!

There were *The Three Bears, Llama, Llama, Fancy Nancy,* and Dr. Seuss!

There were hundreds of Golden Books full of fairy tales and Mother Goose!

There were rhyming books, picture books, and story books, too.

Both children smiled widely as they sat down on a stool.

They began to read and could not get enough.

A stack soon formed; they both loved this stuff!

After a while, Ella frantically jumped up.

She was suddenly worried about their climb up.

She grabbed David and said, "Our mother does not know

that we are here in the clouds, and not down below!"

They thanked the princess for a lovely time,

and down the ladder, they began to climb the long climb.

They climbed and they climbed till they could see down below,

their sandbox and shovels and buckets in a row.

They jumped off the ladder and turned in surprise;

the ladder just disappeared up into the sky!

They kept looking up to where it had been,

but they saw nothing at all. "What happened?" They grinned.

The children were speechless; they couldn't believe their eyes!

Just then, their mother called, "Come on in, you guys!

Dinner is ready, and you need to wash up."

Laughing, they ran to the house in a gallop!

Their mother asked both of them, "Did you find any treasure?"

Both kids smiled. "We sure did!" SAID WITH PLEASURE.

Looking at each other they decided not to tell her.

"We had fun," they both said, "we had fun finding treasure!"

"No eye has seen, no ear has heard, and no mind has imagined what God has prepared for those who love him."

1 Corinthians 2:9

CPSIA information can be obtained
at www.ICGtesting.com
Printed in the USA
LVHW070221150619
621340LV00004B/11/P